Ingredients for a Healthy Life

CREATIVE COCOA Recipes

Gareth Stevens PUBLISHING

By Kristen Rajczak

Please visit our website, www.garethstevens.com. For a free color catalog of all our high-quality books, call toll free 1-800-542-2595 or fax 1-877-542-2596.

Library of Congress Cataloging-in-Publication Data

Rajczak, Kristen.
Creative cocoa recipes / by Kristen Rajczak.
p. cm. — (Ingredients for a healthy life)
Includes index.
ISBN 978-1-4824-3326-5 (pbk.)
ISBN 978-1-4824-3325-8 (6-pack)
ISBN 978-1-4824-0559-0 (library binding)
1. Cooking (Chocolate) — Juvenile literature. 2. Cocoa — Juvenile literature. 3. Chocolate — Juvenile literature. I. Rajczak, Kristen. II. Title.
TX767.C5 N58 2014
641.6—dc23

First Edition

Published in 2015 by
Gareth Stevens Publishing
111 East 14th Street, Suite 349
New York, NY 10003

Designer: Andrea Davison-Bartolotta
Editor: Kristen Rajczak

Photo credits: Cover, back cover, pp. 1, 3, 9, 11, 13, 15, 17, 19, 21–24 (chocolate background) Lossik/Shutterstock.com; cover, p. 1 (hot cocoa) Jaren Jai Wicklund/Shutterstock.com; cover, pp. 1 (cookies, mole), 17 (ingredients), 19, 21 (arrow, boy) iStockphoto/Thinkstock; p. 4 mexrix/Shutterstock.com; p. 5 Comstock Images/Getty Images; p. 7 (map) Serban Bogdan/Shutterstock.com; p. 7 (main) © iStockphoto.com/SPrada; p. 9 Lisa Romerein/FoodPix/Getty Images; p. 10 Valentyn Volkov/Shutterstock.com; p. 11 tacar/Shutterstock.com; p. 13 (bottom) Thomas M Perkins/Shutterstock.com; p. 13 (top) Jenn Huis/Shutterstock.com; p. 15 (bottom) sgm/Shutterstock.com; p. 15 (top) Scruggelgreen/Shutterstock.com; pp. 16, 18 Hemera/Thinkstock; p. 17 (hot cocoa) Elina Manninen/Shutterstock.com; p. 20 Claire Leow/Bloomberg via Getty Images.

Printed in the United States of America

CPSIA compliance information: Batch #CS15GS: For further information contact Gareth Stevens, New York, New York at 1-800-542-2595.

Contents

! Recipes in this book may use knives, mixers, and hot stove tops. Ask for an adult's help when using these tools.

Words in the glossary appear in **bold** type the first time they are used in the text.

Calling All Chocolate Lovers!

Chocolate is surely the best-known product created from the cocoa bean. From cakes and brownies to pudding and hot fudge, cocoa is part of some very tasty desserts! But cocoa isn't actually sweet. The sweetness many people love is due to the sugar that's part of many dessert **recipes**.

By itself, cocoa is good for your body. Read on to learn more about this useful **ingredient** and find some tasty recipes for using cocoa in any meal—including dessert!

Do You Have Allergies?

The recipes in this book may use ingredients that contain or have come into contact with nuts, gluten, dairy products, and other common causes of **allergies**. If you have any food allergies, please ask a parent or teacher for help when cooking and tasting!

Cooking with cocoa can be a fun, healthy activity.

Beans from the Start

A chocolate bar starts as cocoa beans, or seeds of the cacao (kuh-KOW) tree. They're found inside long fruit pods that look a bit like cucumbers. The pods grow on the trunk and branches of the tree. Inside a cocoa bean's hard shell is a little kernel called the nib. The nib is what's used to make cocoa products.

The cacao tree was first grown in South and Central America. Today, it's found in other parts of the world, such as India and Africa.

CHEW ON THIS!

People around the world enjoy the products made from more than 4.4 million tons (4 million mt) of cocoa beans each year.

Cacao trees are commonly grown on small farms within 20 degrees of the **equator**. Use the key from the map above to find where cacao trees are most often grown.

Cocoa Reaches Europe

The Maya, Toltec, and Aztec peoples of Central America were the first to use the fruit of the cacao tree more than 3,000 years ago! When the Spanish explorers arrived during the 1500s, the Aztecs taught them to make a tasty cocoa drink.

Starting around 1600, cocoa drinks became popular across Europe. "Chocolate houses" selling hot cocoa popped up in cities like London, England, during the 1700s. In 1876, a man in Switzerland made the first milk chocolate.

CHEW ON THIS!

Spanish explorers brought cocoa beans back to Spain with them. The Spanish kept the flavorful beans a secret for almost 100 years!

Easy Chicken Mole

Makes 4 servings

Ingredients:

1 1/2 pounds chicken, cut into cubes or strips
4 tablespoons olive oil, divided
1 teaspoon cayenne pepper
1/2 teaspoon black pepper
2 tablespoons chili powder
2 teaspoons cumin
1 teaspoon cinnamon
1 1/2 ounces unsweetened chocolate
4 (14.5-ounce) cans stewed tomatoes

Directions:

1. Mix together black pepper and cayenne pepper in a bowl. Add chicken and toss until it's coated.
2. Heat 2 tablespoons of olive oil in a large pot on the stove top and add the chicken. Cook until the chicken is done, with no pink at its center. Remove chicken with a slotted spoon and set it aside.
3. Mix chili powder with cumin and cinnamon, and add more cayenne pepper and black pepper if you want the sauce to be spicier.
4. Heat 2 tablespoons of olive oil in the same pot and add the chili powder mix. Stir the spices and oil with a spoon for about 6 minutes, or until the mixture is blackened and hot.
5. Lower the stove top's heat. Add the chocolate, and stir until it's melted. Add the stewed tomatoes and bring the mixture to a boil. Stir well.
6. After about 10 minutes, put the chicken back in the pot. Continue cooking until heated through, about 5 minutes. Serve warm.

Mole (MOH-lay) is a sauce often used in Mexican **cuisine**. Making a traditional mole usually takes a lot of time and many ingredients. This recipe copies these flavors and makes them a little simpler so your family can make it anytime!

Health Halo

One reason cocoa became so popular in Europe was that it was known as a "health-giving" food among the wealthy. Today, scientists have found this to be true!

Cocoa powder has a high amount of **antioxidants**. It may keep your heart healthier by helping you maintain lower blood pressure. Cocoa contains healthy **fats** and has been said to lower the risk of some illnesses. Using cocoa powder and eating small amounts of dark chocolate are the best ways to gain cocoa's health benefits.

CHEW ON THIS!

When cocoa is mixed with lots of sugar and other not-so-healthy additions—such as marshmallows or cookies—its **nutritional value** is less. Enjoy these treats, but only a little at a time!

cocoa pod

Cocoa Almond Granola

makes about 12 cups of cereal

Ingredients:

8 cups quick-cooking oats
1 cup sliced toasted almonds
2 cups unsweetened coconut
1/2 cup light butter
3/4 cup real maple syrup
1/4 cup unsweetened cocoa powder
1/2 tablespoon vanilla extract

Directions:

1. Preheat the oven to 250 degrees.
2. Combine oats, almonds, and coconut in a large bowl. Stir together.
3. Melt butter in a small measuring cup. Add the maple syrup and cocoa powder. Stir together and microwave for about 30 seconds, or until the mixture is smooth. Add the vanilla.
4. Pour the maple syrup mixture over the bowl of oats, almonds, and coconut. Stir so the dry ingredients are coated.
5. Spread the mixture onto two cookie sheets. Bake at 250 degrees for 30 minutes. Use a spatula to turn the granola, then bake for another 30 minutes, or until golden brown.
6. Allow to cool. Store in an airtight container.

Store-bought cereals can have a lot of added sugar. Make this easy recipe for a more healthful—and chocolaty—breakfast, or use it to top yogurt or ice cream!

Chocolate, Simply

Cocoa beans are specially **processed** in order to become cocoa powder or chocolate. First, the fruit of the cacao tree is picked and the beans removed. Then, the beans are put into leaf-lined holes in the ground or shallow boxes for about a week to lose water and **ferment**.

The beans are dried and roasted. The nibs are then ground to release the fat in them—cocoa butter—and form a paste called chocolate liquor, or cocoa mass. Cocoa butter might be pressed out to make cocoa powder, or more cocoa butter may be added to make chocolate candy.

CHEW ON THIS!

Beyond the basic process, different places have their own way of making chocolate. Belgian chocolate makers, for example, receive the main chocolate-making ingredient as a liquid in a tank on a truck, while many others have it delivered in solid form.

Chocolate Chip Cookies

To make chocolate, such as the chips used in this recipe, sugar and sometimes milk or other flavors are added to the chocolate liquor. Use whatever kind of chip is your favorite!

Ingredients:

2 1/4 cups flour
1 teaspoon baking soda
1/4 teaspoon salt
3/4 cup brown sugar
1/2 cup white sugar
1/2 cup light butter
1 teaspoon vanilla extract
2 egg whites
3/4 cup chocolate chips

Directions:

1. Preheat oven to 350 degrees. Line cookie sheets with parchment paper or lightly coat with cooking spray.
2. Combine flour, baking soda, and salt in a bowl. Mix together with a fork or whisk.
3. Microwave butter until just soft, about 15 to 30 seconds. Add it to a large bowl with both kinds of sugar. Mix well.
4. Separate your eggs. Then, add the whites to the butter and sugar mixture. Mix in the vanilla, too.
5. A little at a time, blend in the flour mixture until the batter is smooth.
6. Mix in the chocolate chips.
7. Use a spoon to scoop the batter onto the cookie sheets, leaving a couple of inches between each cookie.
8. Bake for 10 minutes, or until lightly browned.
9. Allow cookies to cool for 2 minutes before removing from the sheet.
10. Repeat with remaining batter.

Kinds of Chocolate

There seems to be no end to the variety of chocolate! Here are some common types:

- **unsweetened/baking chocolate:** Often used for baking, it's pure chocolate liquor with no sugar added, so it tastes bitter.
- **milk chocolate:** Cocoa butter and chocolate liquor make up the base of it, but it also actually has milk in it! In the United States, it's usually dried milk.
- **dark chocolate:** It's less sweet than milk chocolate, though it does contain sugar and vanilla. What sets dark chocolate apart is the high cocoa content, commonly 30 to 80 percent!

CHEW ON THIS!

Is it chocolate if there's no cocoa in it? White chocolate is made of cocoa butter but not the cocoa solids in chocolate liquor, so it tastes like vanilla or other flavors it might be made with.

Nutty Chocolate Frosting

makes about 1/2 cup

Ingredients:

1/4 cup peanut butter
4 teaspoons pure maple syrup
2 tablespoons cocoa powder
4 teaspoons milk (or a bit more if you want a thinner result)
3/4 teaspoon pure vanilla extract

Directions:

1. Use a fork to mix all the ingredients together.
2. Chill in a covered bowl in the fridge until you want to use it.

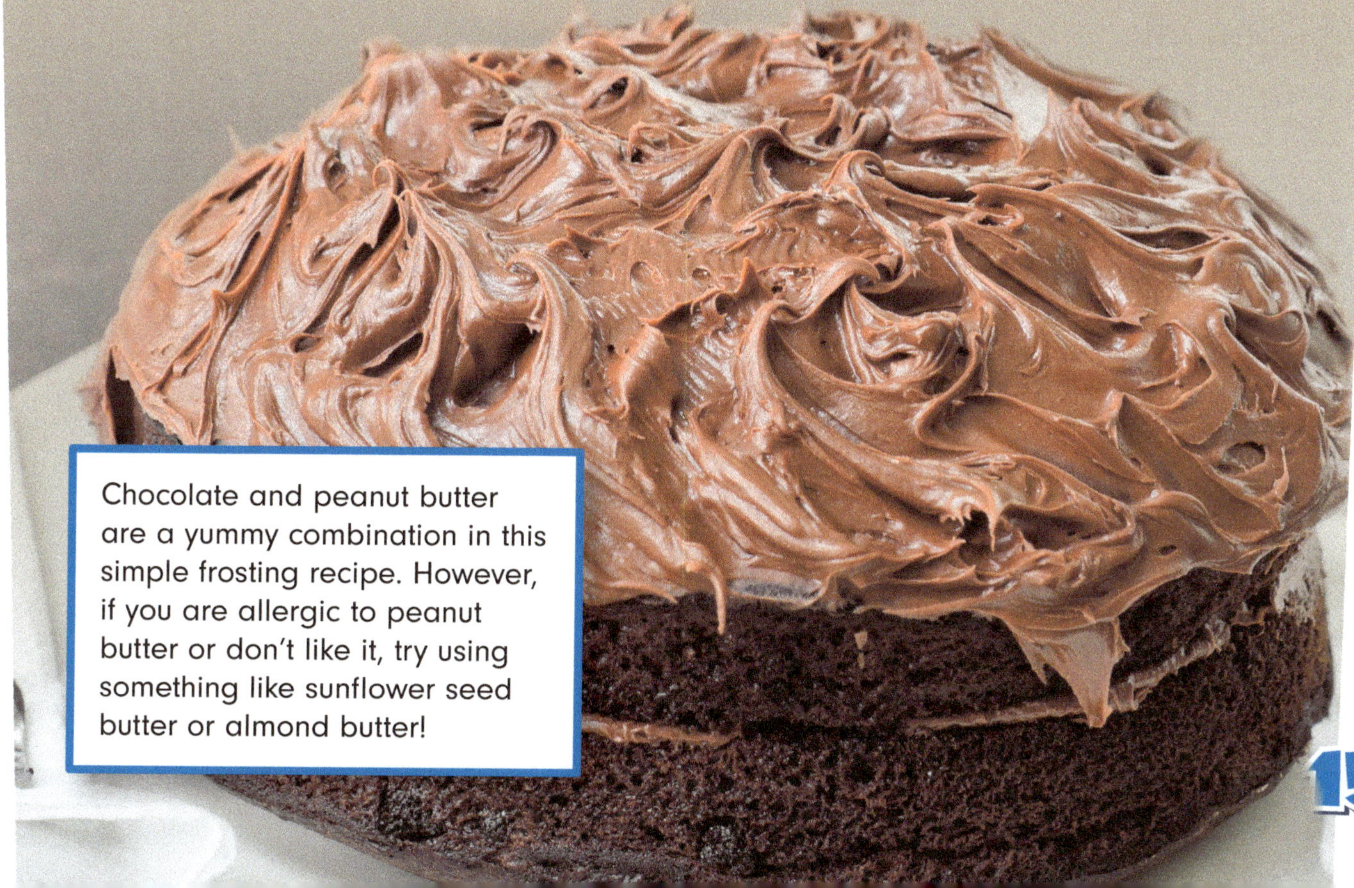

Chocolate and peanut butter are a yummy combination in this simple frosting recipe. However, if you are allergic to peanut butter or don't like it, try using something like sunflower seed butter or almond butter!

Sweet Additions

Do you know what kind of chocolate you like? Melt it, and make your own candy! First, place the chocolate in a microwave-safe bowl. Then, microwave it for about 30 seconds at a time and stir. When it's smooth, mix in your favorite chocolate pairings and either spread on a cookie sheet or spoon into a minimuffin tin and freeze it.

Some healthy—and yummy—mix-ins could be raisins or other dried fruit, nuts, coconut flakes, or even cereal!

CHEW ON THIS!

The chocolate made for candy coating often has vegetable oil in it instead of cocoa butter to make it melt more easily. However, it often won't have as strong a chocolate flavor.

milk chocolate and dark chocolate with pecans

Hot Cocoa from Scratch

makes 4 servings

Ingredients:

4 cups milk
4 tablespoons unsweetened cocoa
4 tablespoons honey
cinnamon (optional)

Directions:

1. Measure milk into a medium pan and place on the stove top.
2. Heat the milk on low until it just starts to boil.
3. Add the cocoa and honey to the milk. Mix until they are well combined.
4. Pour into mugs. Sprinkle cinnamon on top for a fun flavor twist!

There's no need to rip open a packet in this recipe! Ask an adult for help using the stove top to make some great hot cocoa to share.

Chocolate for Dinner?

Have you ever seen pasta with a chocolate sauce? Or a chocolate bar with bacon in it? Some people even eat sandwiches made with chocolate and cheese. And the famous chili often served over spaghetti in Cincinnati, Ohio, commonly has a secret ingredient—cocoa!

Cocoa's flavor pairs well with many spices, such as cinnamon and chili pepper, and it's often in spice rubs for meats like pork. Cocoa can add a special taste to your favorite meal!

beef with chocolate chili sauce

CHEW ON THIS!

The cocoa bean is used for more than just food. Cocoa butter is often used to heal dry skin and chapped lips.

Choco-Coffee Barbeque Sauce

Did you know cocoa goes well with meat? Use this tasty barbeque sauce at your next picnic!

Ingredients:

2 tablespoons olive oil
1 onion, diced
4 large garlic cloves, chopped
2 tablespoons chili powder
1 tablespoon cumin
1 teaspoon coriander
1/4 teaspoon cinnamon
1 tablespoon unsweetened cocoa powder
1 cup plain tomato sauce
1/2 cup brown sugar
1 cup brewed decaf coffee (or 1 tablespoon instant decaf coffee and 1 cup water)
1/2 cup red wine vinegar
2 tablespoons Worcestershire sauce
1/4 cup molasses
1 tablespoon yellow mustard
salt and pepper

Directions:

1. Heat the olive oil in a medium pan on the stove top. Add the onion and garlic, and coat them with the hot oil. Stir until the onions are soft.
2. Stir in the chili powder, cumin, coriander, cinnamon, and cocoa, and cook for about 1 minute.
3. Add the tomato sauce and brown sugar, and cook, stirring until fully combined, about 2 minutes.
4. Stir in the decaf coffee, vinegar, Worcestershire sauce, molasses, and mustard.
5. Keep the stove top on low for about 25 minutes until the sauce thickens.
6. Allow the sauce to cool. Use immediately on your favorite barbeque items, or cover and store in the fridge.

Fair Trade

When you're considering the health benefits of cocoa, thinking about the health of others and the world around you is a good idea. Some cocoa is "fair trade." This means the cocoa bean farmers have been paid fairly for their crops, and those who worked on the product were treated well and paid enough.

Fair trade practices let farmers and cocoa processors use the best, local methods for making cocoa. Many people think fair trade chocolate tastes better because of this!

cocoa farm

Healthy Reasons to Choose Cocoa

Eating cocoa has been shown to cause the brain to make the substances that boost mood and happiness.

The antioxidants in cocoa—flavanols—are said to lower blood pressure and improve blood flow to the brain and heart.

The healthy fat in cocoa has lots of benefits, including helping us feel full longer.

Cocoa contains caffeine, which helps you feel energized and awake to run and play.

Glossary

allergy: a body's sensitivity to usually harmless things in the surroundings, such as dust, pollen, or mold

antioxidant: a substance that helps the body repair itself

cuisine: a style of cooking

equator: an imaginary line around Earth that is the same distance from the North and the South Poles

fat: one of the basic nutrients that supply energy to the body

ferment: to change a sugar or starch into an alcohol or acid in the absence of oxygen

ingredient: a food that is mixed with other foods

nutritional value: the makeup of a food and its impact on the body

process: to move something forward in a set of steps. Also, the set of steps itself.

recipe: an explanation of how to make a food

For More Information

BOOKS

Kuskowski, Alex. *Cool Eating: Healthy & Fun Ways to Eat Right*. Minneapolis, MN: ABDO Publishing, 2013.

Malam, John. *Journey of a Bar of Chocolate*. Chicago, IL: Heinemann Library, 2013.

WEBSITES

All About Chocolate: Just for Kids
archive.fieldmuseum.org/chocolate/kids.html
Find out more about how chocolate is made, and play games about what you learn.

Kids Health: Recipes and Cooking
kidshealth.org/kid/recipes/
This recipe website for kids has lots of fun recipes to make, even for those with food allergies or other health issues.

Publisher's note to educators and parents: Our editors have carefully reviewed these websites to ensure that they are suitable for students. Many websites change frequently, however, and we cannot guarantee that a site's future contents will continue to meet our high standards of quality and educational value. Be advised that students should be closely supervised whenever they access the Internet.

Index